SAFE RETURN

For my father, Ward Dexter

First edition 1996

Library of Congress Cataloging-in-Publication Data is available.
ISBN 0-7636-0005-9

2 4 6 8 10 9 7 5 3 1

Printed in the United States

This book was typeset in Centaur MT.

Candlewick Press
2067 Massachusetts Avenue
Cambridge, MA 02140

SAFE RETURN

Catherine
Dexter

CANDLEWICK PRESS
CAMBRIDGE, MASSACHUSETTS

CHAPTER ONE

Early that morning I went down the harbor road to my favorite rock and climbed up on it so I could check on the ship. I wasn't exactly hoping it had sunk in the night, but maybe it would have just mysteriously disappeared.

There it was, though. I could see the tops of its masts bobbing cheerfully up and down in the harbor.

I sat down for a moment. There's a dip in the top of the rock where I just fit, like a cup in its saucer, and I like to sit there and look out as far as I can, over the harbor and out to the open sea. The sun was flashing on the water, and I took a deep breath of the salt air. I love that smell. I even like the smell of seaweed washed up on the shore, though it makes some people hold their nose. But that day the salt air made me shiver, and all I could think of was how deep the sea really was.

The next day my aunt Dana and nine other women from our island were going to sail on the *Galatina* to Stockholm, over a hundred miles away. They were taking along hundreds of sweaters that they and other people had knitted to sell in the marketplace. They do this every year, and they're always home in plenty of time for Christmas. It had never bothered me before when Aunt Dana went on this trip, and I didn't know why I was worried about it now. I kept hoping something would happen so she'd have to stay home.

I had promised Aunt Dana I wouldn't be gone long, so I gave a big leap from my rock to the ground. Then I ran for home, cutting across some fields where sheep were standing around nibbling grass. One of them looked up at me with its mouth full, the green ends sticking out on both sides like whiskers. I stopped and dug my fingers into its shaggy back, a thick, good handful. I like the way sheep smell, too — grass and wool and a whiff of manure. Then I ran the rest of the way. When something is wrong, I always feel better after I start running.

I could see the Gunderssons' cart and horse tied up by the door of our cottage. I dodged around it and ran in. "I'm back!" I shouted. A chair fell over. Aunt Dana and Marta Gundersson turned from the mountains of sweaters heaped on the floor and the table and the bench by the wall.

"So we see," said Aunt Dana. I picked up the chair and set it back on its legs. "Ursula, look at this beautiful hat that Marta made." She held up a creamy white cap with red roses and green ivy swirling around the rim. "See how the roses go to the left, all the way around? You must always have the pattern going clockwise. Otherwise, it's bad luck."

Always? When was I ever going to knit at all, never mind going to the left or to the right? Everyone on this island can knit, even men, even children; everyone but me. Aunt Dana has tried to teach me lots of times, but I haven't learned. I have a tangle of knitting hidden up in my cupboard from the last time.

"And look inside." Aunt Dana turned back the rim of the cap. "No knots at all."

"Mmm, yes," I said.

"Knots are bad luck, too," said Marta.

As if I didn't already know that.

Once, last spring, I overheard Marta telling Aunt Dana that it was time I learned to knit, that everyone had to knit, that I was eleven years old now — much too old not to know how — think of how useful I could make myself.

"She'll learn one day," Aunt Dana had answered.

"You have to insist on it." Marta likes to give advice. "If she were your own child, you wouldn't go so soft on her."

"I'm sure you're right," said Aunt Dana in a cool pleasant voice that meant, *I'll do what I like.*

"Where are Annelise and Peter?" I asked Marta. Annelise Gundersson is twelve years old, and her brother, Peter, is six. Annelise is so good at knitting she can walk around and knit at the same time. Sometimes she knits while she's walking to school, like the older girls do. Peter has a set of needles, too, but I'm pretty sure he's never used them.

"Annelise is home watching the dye pot," said Marta. "And Peter went down to the dock to look at the ship. He'll make sure it's good and safe for you, Dana!" Both of them laughed. "We'll pray for good weather," Marta added. I wished she hadn't said that. Aunt Dana says October is the busiest time for the market, the best time to sell things, but everyone knows it's not the best time to cross the Baltic Sea. Autumn storms can be dangerous.

"Take these with you," said Aunt Dana, and she handed Marta a basket lined with a cloth. Inside were warm saffron rolls she had baked that morning. "Josef will bring back the cart tomorrow."

I watched Marta start walking up the path toward their farm. It's a mile or so away. I can run all the way there without stopping for breath. Maybe Annelise can knit, but she can't run as far or as fast as I can.

Aunt Dana wrapped more rolls and some cheese in a

napkin. "Go out to the barn now," she said. "Tell Josef the sooner we go, the better." The Gunderssons had lent us their cart so that we could go around and collect the last of the knitted things Aunt Dana was taking to Stockholm.

Uncle Josef was sitting on a milking stool repairing a gate to one of the barn stalls. Uncle Josef and Aunt Dana own two cows and twenty chickens and six hundred sheep.

"Aunt Dana says it's time to go," I told him. "Will you let me drive? Will you?"

Uncle Josef went on fitting the wooden slat into the gate frame without saying a thing. When he had finished, he looked over at me — his back is a little bit crooked, so he held his head to one side. "Think you can drive, do you?" he said. He pulled himself to his feet and limped across the barn floor to put his tools away. "Well, we'll see."

That meant yes. I would have hugged him if he had been Aunt Dana, but since he wasn't, I said, "Goody!" and clapped my hands and tried not to squeal. Then I ran back to help Aunt Dana. We spread an old quilt on the floor of the cart, so the sweaters would stay clean, and we put our lunch into a basket and closed the cottage door. Uncle Josef shut up the barn. Then we climbed into the cart. It started forward with a creak and a jerk, and Aunt Dana took out her knitting; she takes it with her wherever she goes. She was making a gray stocking. Her fingers work so fast you can't see her take any single stitch.

As soon as we had reached the level road that leads to the Hansons' farm, Uncle Josef handed me the reins. "Nice and easy," he said. "Remember how you did it last time."

I love holding the worn leather reins and feeling Bruno pull against them. His backside always looks three times larger when I'm the one who's driving. I pulled on one rein to guide him toward the center of the road.

"You've a good hand," said Uncle Josef. Aunt Dana looked around me at Uncle Josef and nodded. I knew they were pleased with me.

"You two will get along nicely while I'm gone," said Aunt Dana. "This is going to be our best trip ever. The

wool is exceptionally good this year. It's very soft."
Her dark eyes sparkled and her cheeks turned pink.
She didn't seem the least bit worried. "Last year I
saw a man with a gold birdcage, and there were two
birds in it, and they talked," she said. "Who knows
what there'll be this year."

I hadn't noticed, but Bruno's pace had picked up.
Uncle Josef put his hands over mine and together we
pulled back — slowly, steadily — on the reins.

"Are you sure you'll be home in time for Christmas?" I asked. She had told me this before, but I
wanted to hear her say it again.

"Oh, long before Christmas. We'll be gone four
weeks all told," said Aunt Dana. "We'll be back by the
middle of November."

"And will the man with the red candles be there?"
I asked.

"He always is. And last year there was someone
selling velvet cloaks. I saw pearl necklaces, and a sil-
versmith with a tray of belt buckles, and a troop of
dancers from Spain."

It was time to turn up the Hansons' path. "Whoa

there," I said, this time pulling back all on my own. You need a steady touch, Uncle Josef says. No jerking. The cart came to a smooth halt.

Aunt Dana climbed down as Helga Hanson came out to greet us. Tucked in the crook of Helga's arm was her new baby. It was crying.

"Hey, now, you hold him for me." She reached up and put the baby into my arms. He was wrapped tightly in a white shawl. I looked down at his small dusky head, his eyes squeezed shut, his pink mouth opening and closing with shivery little screams coming out. "Wants his lunch," said Helga, and she and Aunt Dana disappeared into the house.

I jiggled the baby up and down, which seemed to make him scream louder, and then he fell asleep, just like that.

In a moment Helga and Aunt Dana emerged from the cottage with their arms full of sweaters and stockings. They laid them in the cart. Helga took back her baby and stepped to one side of the path. "Safe journey!" she called out. The baby startled awake and began to wail again.

"Why doesn't Helga go?" I asked as Uncle Josef nudged the cart forward.

"She can't leave her baby," said Aunt Dana.

"Why not?"

"He's too young."

"Why?"

"Infants must stay with their mothers."

"Marta doesn't go," I said. "Is that because she can't leave her children?"

"Perhaps."

"Why can't she leave them?"

"Perhaps she can, but she chooses not to."

"But you always go."

Aunt Dana gave me a long look. "I go, and Ella Helfrigs goes, and Sonja Wilhelmsson; and their children stay behind. I've gone every year, Ursula, and you and Uncle Josef always get along fine without me. I wonder what's making you ask these things now."

I didn't know what was making me ask these things now.

When we reached the road again, I stood up and turned around to wave good-bye to Gerta. For a moment I tried pretending I was the one setting out for the mainland; I was in charge of all these beautiful sweaters and would sail on the ship myself and take everything to the market.

But I couldn't imagine it. Instead, a hollow feeling settled in my stomach and wouldn't go away.

CHAPTER TWO

That night we tied all the sweaters into bundles with cords made of twisted yarn. Then we sat near the stove, putting off the time for going to bed. Aunt Dana had finished the gray stocking and started on another, and Uncle Josef was working on a sweater with a pattern of dark birds in the yoke. The creamy wool and the dark strands moved quickly through his big gnarled fingers, alternating, now the light yarn on top, now the black.

"What are those?" I asked him.

"Gulls," he said. "Gulls mean land close by."

"Are they going around like this?" I drew a circle in the air, going to the left.

Uncle Josef nodded.

"Why?" I asked. "Why does it have to go that way?"

"Ursula, you're full of questions tonight," said Aunt Dana. She looked over at Uncle Josef. "Tell the story about Ole."

He smiled and shook his head.

"Go on, tell it," she urged.

"Well, then," he began. "Once there was a very old man, and he wore a very old cap. It wore out, so he needed a new one. It must be knitted by a young girl, so that he would live longer. It must be made of gray and black wool from the youngest sheep. It must have a pattern in the border, and a striped crown, and a tassel hanging down to here." He pointed to the top of his ear. "But when it was done, exactly as the old man had ordered it, he refused to wear it. The girl had knit the wheels in the border going the wrong way round. He believed he would never get to heaven if he wore that cap."

Whenever I heard this story, I wondered how the girl had felt when she found out she had done it wrong. "Do you think he would have gone to heaven anyway?" I asked.

"Probably not," said Uncle Josef.

Aunt Dana laughed, as if she didn't take these things so seriously.

"How long does it take to sail to Stockholm?" I asked.

"Does that make a hundred times you've asked that question?" said Aunt Dana. "Two and a half days in good weather."

"And how long in bad weather?"

"As long as it takes," said Aunt Dana. "Do you remember when you crossed the sea?"

I was waiting for her to ask me that. "I only remember when we left," I said. I had told my part of the story many times. "We went on board, and the ship was rolling and rolling, it was so windy, and Mrs. Swenson picked me up because the deck was going up and down. I saw the dock and the land get smaller and smaller — I didn't realize we were sailing, I thought they were moving the land away so we couldn't get back to it. I stared down at Mrs. Swenson's sweater, at the crisscross lines and flowers, and I never looked up again until we went below."

"And two days later, Mrs. Swenson brought you to our door," Aunt Dana continued the story. "'A terrible fever has gone through Stockholm,' Mrs. Swenson said. 'Your sister and her husband have died, and I've brought you their girl. I am so sorry.' And there you were, my sister's only child, an orphan. You belonged with us from that moment on."

"And tell the part about how my mother knew you were going to take me," I said.

Aunt Dana nodded. "She and I were as close as this when we were children on the farm." She held up two fingers pressed together. "After I married Josef and came to this island, we wrote to each other, and I saw her every fall when I went to Stockholm. I even held you when you were a baby, though of course you can't remember that. I have always been sure that no matter how sick she was, she knew that we would take you in, and your father would also have known."

"And that night we all sat up," I went on.

"Yes, everyone came to our house and stayed until late into the night."

Then Aunt Dana stopped talking, and I remembered silently, too. On that first evening people kept coming to the cottage. Men and women sat in a circle all around the main room, knitting. They talked and told stories and laughed and sometimes looked over at me where I sat huddled up on a wooden stool between Mrs. Swenson and Aunt Dana. I didn't know anyone but Mrs. Swenson — I didn't even know my aunt — and the room was hot and close with the smell of stove smoke and greasy wool and strangers' clothes.

Then the door opened and a woman wearing a cloak stepped into the room and threw back her hood. I glimpsed a rosy face and brown hair caught smoothly at the nape of her neck. It was my mother! The woman came across the room and bent down to greet me, and it was someone I didn't know.

Pretty soon she will really come, I thought. That was nearly her.

I waited all night for her. I waited while everyone else was knitting and talking and laughing as if nothing was wrong.

In the morning Mrs. Swenson left, and Aunt Dana told me again that my mother and father had died; but I thought she had made a mistake, or I hadn't heard right. Maybe Mrs. Swenson was going to send my mother and father back to the island. I didn't want to make it not happen because I had forgotten to wait for them. I still kept waiting, though I didn't say so. But as long as I waited, she never came. And when I got a bit older, I understood what it meant that she had died, and my father, too.

"We can't stay up any later tonight," Aunt Dana said now. "I have to finish packing in the morning."

"What if there's a storm?" I asked. "If there's a storm tomorrow, the ship won't leave, will it?"

"Of course not," said Aunt Dana. "But the sky was clear at sunset. There's fine weather ahead."

CHAPTER THREE

The next morning Aunt Dana was up early, even for her. I lay in bed listening to the rustling noises below. Then I climbed down to watch her pack her big tapestry traveling bag. In went clean clothes and a nightgown and some food for the journey — cheese and dried fish and hard-boiled eggs and bread — and her hairbrush. Uncle Josef was setting the table for breakfast.

"Let me see — my wallet!" Aunt Dana had a leather pouch fitted on a belt for the money she was going to collect. "I'll sleep with this around my waist every night. No one can steal it without stealing me, too." She stepped to the door of the cottage. "It's a beautiful day, beautiful!"

I looked out beside her. It *was* a glorious day —

the sky was bright, a clean wind blew — there was absolutely no chance the sailing would be postponed. In the distance I heard the creaking of the Gunderssons' cart, and then it came into view beyond a grove of trees.

"There they are!" I shrieked and flung my arms around my aunt.

"Now, then." Aunt Dana laughed and gently pushed me away.

"We'll bring the cart back tonight," said Uncle Josef as Hans climbed down.

"That'll be fine," said Hans. "And a good journey to you, Dana," he said as he set off on foot for home.

We went inside and sat around the table and ate bread, boiled eggs, salted fish, and bowls of porridge and milk with honey swirled on top. Uncle Josef had cooked a real traveler's breakfast so Aunt Dana wouldn't get hungry all day. But my stomach was in a knot, and I could get down only a few bites.

After we had finished eating, we carried the bundles of sweaters to the cart, and then there was nothing to do but drive down to Visby to the harbor.

Other families were gathering on the wharf, and the sweater ladies were arranging their cargoes of knitting at the foot of the gangplank. Children raced each other up and down the dock while their parents scurried around, calling to one another and shouting directions and reminders. I could tell I was the only one who was dreading having the ship leave.

I jumped down from the cart and went across the splintery wharf to where the ship was anchored. Up close, the *Galatina* was huge. Sailors darted around on her deck, shouting things. Waves slapped at her keel, and ropes and boards thudded and groaned as the ship rode up and down. What did that creaking mean? Was something coming apart? Had anyone gone down to the bottom of the ship to see?

Uncle Josef was helping Aunt Dana lift down the bundles of knitting from the cart. No one seemed to notice the groaning of the ship. It was going to be loaded and leave port, no matter what. This would happen, and there was nothing I could do. Aunt Dana was walking straight to her doom. She was going to die.

Ella Helfrigs was standing on the dock beside her

bundles of knitting. She kept calling out to her two children to stop their foolish running, they could fall right in and drown. I knew Gunnar and Greta from school. Greta is a year younger than I am, and Gunnar is two years older. Their father was a fisherman, lost at sea many years ago. Their mother makes a fine living with her knitting, Aunt Dana said.

They ignored their mother and ran up to me. Greta caught my hand. "Come on, Ursula, run with us!"

I shook my head.

"Why not? What's the matter?" Greta peered into my face. "Are you going to cry?" She kept holding my hand.

Gunnar's big freckled face loomed over me. "It's just your aunt who's going," he put in. He was big for his age, and rough spoken. "She's not your mother."

I hated Gunnar right then. I was choking with what I wanted to say —*My aunt is just as good as your mother. She's just as good as anyone's mother.* But I couldn't speak.

"Well, stand there, then," said Greta, and she let go of my hand and took off, her short blonde braids flying out behind her.

"Crybaby!" Gunnar shouted at me as he ran after Greta.

I took a deep breath. *You've always been fine before*, Aunt Dana had told me. *You and Uncle Josef will get along just fine.*

Now Aunt Dana was talking to a sailor, who hoisted several of her bundles onto his shoulder. He carried them up the gangplank onto the ship. Aunt Dana herself carried one bundle aboard, then came back for the rest. She laughed as the wind caught her shawl and flapped it up over her head.

The wind whipped at my skirt. *You will be fine.* I made myself think it in Aunt Dana's voice. And for a moment the cries of the wheeling gulls and the shouts of the sailors and even the ship itself, riding the water impatiently, all seemed good. This was an adventure, it would be all right, people crossed the sea safely all the time.

Then, before I knew it, it was time for good-byes. I put my arms around Aunt Dana's broad waist and squeezed. She hugged me extra long. "I'll be back sooner than you think. Four Sundays, that's all. You'll remember to do your chores, won't you? And try to guess what I'll bring you." She turned to Uncle Josef, and they hugged and clasped hands without saying anything.

Now Aunt Dana was climbing the slanting gangplank. A moment later she peeped over the railing of the main deck and waved to us. She was so high up, she didn't seem to belong to us anymore.

I reached for Uncle Josef's hand.

Sailors shouted; ropes were hauled up. The gangplank was hoisted away. Sailors scampered up the masts and the rigging and began to unfurl the sails. The sails flapped and steadied and caught the beginnings of a breeze. Slowly the ship moved away from the dock.

"Can we stay and watch till they're all the way gone?" I asked. I was still gripping Uncle Josef's hand so hard my fingers hurt.

Uncle Josef shook his head. "It's bad luck," he said. "Now they must go on their way, and we must go on ours." He put his hand on my shoulder and steered me away from the water's edge. As we crossed the wharf

I couldn't help but look back once or twice to see how far away the ship had gotten. I was hoping that didn't count as bad luck.

That afternoon Uncle Josef said I could drive the cart back to the Gunderssons' by myself. I was careful to pay attention to what I was doing the whole way so that Bruno didn't take on a mind of his own. When I was concentrating on driving, I didn't have room in my head to worry about Aunt Dana.

I brought the cart to a neat halt in front of the Gunderssons' house.

"What a good driver you are!" said Hans Gundersson as he came out. Annelise and Peter crowded after him. Hans held the horse so I could jump down.

"When can I drive the cart?" asked Annelise. "Ursula's only eleven!"

"And me! I want to drive the cart!" said Peter.

"As soon as you're not afraid of the horse," said their father.

"Ursula, come in for a minute," Marta called from

the door. I stepped in and smelled bread baking. You always smell that at their house. Marta handed me a hot cinnamon twist, and right away I started to feel lonesome. There was their whole family, together. "Now you must tell me if you need anything in the days ahead," said Marta. "The time will go fast. Come to our house anytime you want to. And you should keep those little hands busy while your aunt is gone."

"Oh, yes," I said, and started to back away. I knew she would help us anytime we needed it, but I didn't want her to get too motherish right now. "Don't forget to stop for me tomorrow on the way to school," I said to Peter and Annelise. "Good-bye!" I backed out the door and ran for home, holding the uneaten cinnamon twist.

Aunt Dana had left some soup for our supper that first night. I put that on the back of the stove to heat up, and then I set two places at the table. There was a gap of bare wood where Aunt Dana usually sat.

Uncle Josef came in from the barn to eat. Our spoons made little plinking noises against the bowls, and I listened to Uncle Josef slurp and swallow. Usually Aunt Dana did most of the talking. Burning wood crackled. There was a mellow roar as a draft sucked air up the stove chimney.

I still wasn't hungry.

"Do I have to go to school tomorrow?" I said. I would rather have stayed in the cottage, curled up like a hibernating bear; or why not go around with Uncle Josef all day as he tended the animals?

Uncle Josef scraped the last of the soup from his bowl and looked up at me.

"Why do I have to go? I can read. I can do sums."

"Children go to school," he said, the way you would say "Cows eat grass" or "Stones sink in the sea."

If only I could have said how hollow I felt right then, as dark began to swallow the cottage, making the center smaller and smaller, until it was just a yellow glow from the front of the stove. But people keep such things to themselves. Uncle Josef's face was remote as he pulled on his clay pipe, and I watched my hands turn pink as I held them close to the fire.

CHAPTER FOUR

The next morning Annelise and Peter knocked on the door, and I walked with them down the harbor road to school. As we got near the white wooden building, I saw Gunnar and Greta pushing at each other on the path, squabbling over who got to carry their lunch pail. Gunnar looked up when he saw me.

"There's the crybaby," he boomed, losing interest in the lunch pail. He gave Greta a shove and stalked toward me. "Still sniffling?" He rubbed his eyes and pretended to bawl.

"Get away, Gunnar," said Annelise.

I followed her into the schoolhouse. A few children had already come inside, and I looked for the ones whose mothers had gone on the ship. There was Inga

Wilhelmsson, and Nils Ekstrom, and the twins Frida and Karin Olson. They were only eight years old, but they were knitting socks for their little sister. Of course, each of them had to knit only one sock in order to get a pair. Their granny lived with them and took care of them while their mother was gone. They didn't look any different from their usual selves.

I took my place. After all the children had come into the room, Miss Nordstrom shut the door, closing out the sky. Then she smiled, as if we were a herd of lost calves she had just recaptured and locked into the barn.

We ate our lunches on the schoolhouse steps that day because the weather was so fine. No one mention-ed the ship. But Nils Ekstrom began to brag. He said his mother had made two whole sweaters in one day last summer, and so she had to be the fastest knitter on earth.

"That's nothing," said Inga Wilhelmsson. "My mother has six black sheep, and their wool is so light, it's as light as cobwebs, and it's magic, too, because it will never break!"

"Not ever?" asked Frida Olson.

"I'm going to ask Mama if that's true," said Karin Olson.

"How can you? She's gone," said Hanna Lundborg.

Everyone fell silent, and then Miss Nordstrom said, "There are no knitters like our knitters, are there? And no wool like our wool."

Annelise and Peter walked home with me after school, too. Annelise made Peter carry their books and lunch pail while she walked along knitting around and around on a dark brown sock. Annelise was turning into such a little grownup. She fussed at Peter — "Watch the rock there! Don't trip!" She looked like her mother, too, walking along and talking and holding out her elbows so she could keep the knitting needles working.

"Mama says your aunt will probably write to you," she told me. "Though you may not get the letter, as there might not be a ship coming in for a while."

We had reached our cottage, and we stood outside.

"I don't care," I said. "My aunt's going to bring me

a present. She might bring me a birdcage with a yellow and green bird in it." I wasn't too sure about the yellow and green, but I liked the way it sounded.

"Mmm," said Annelise.

"Don't you believe me?" I said.

"A birdcage?" Peter repeated.

"A golden birdcage," I said. "With a pair of birds. And the birds can talk."

"That's nice," said Annelise.

"And maybe she'll get me a pearl necklace, too, and a velvet cloak from Spain."

"Really?"

"Yes, *really!* She saw everything last year."

"But how does she know it will be there this year?" asked Peter.

"She knows. They always have the same things, every year," I said. "She's going to bring me candy. Peppermint drops. And red candles for Christmas."

"We have only white ones," said Annelise.

"You have to go to Stockholm to get red candles," I said.

Annelise gave me a tolerant smile, as if she didn't

believe a word I said, and she and Peter continued down the road.

I stepped into the cottage. "Uncle Josef?" I called. No answer. "Uncle Josef?" I went and stood at the foot of the ladder going up to my sleeping loft, though I knew he wasn't up there. He must be out in the barn or walking across a field somewhere. Of course he wouldn't be far away.

A funny feeling came into my bones. I knew there would be times like this when I didn't know where he was. I knew I would have to spend some time by myself. But it would be all right.

In the silence of the house I heard ringing in my ears.

I left my books on the table and ran outside to the barnyard. I stood on the lowest rung of the fence and watched the chickens for a while until I felt better. They clucked and squawked and scolded and ruffled their rust brown feathers over nothing I could see. They reminded me of Annelise and Marta.

The next morning Gunnar was waiting for me near the schoolhouse door. Dread shot through me the moment I caught sight of him with his shock of yellow hair and his big boots. Gunnar is tall and has great big feet.

"How's the crybaby today?" he teased as I started up the steps. My face turned hot, and the crying started to well up. I held my breath, but I could feel my face crumpling and tears wetting my eyes. I managed to stop, but not before Gunnar saw. He pointed and laughed.

Greta was coming up the steps behind me, and she said, "Gunnar, let her be." Annelise gave him a disgusted look. He galloped away on his long ugly legs. I noticed he didn't go over to the others to see if he could make them cry.

I stayed indoors to eat my lunch that day. I knew if I was slow leaving the schoolroom at the end of the day, I wouldn't have to see Gunnar again. Gunnar and Greta had to go right home, because their aged aunt stayed with them when their mother was gone, and she couldn't do many chores. So that's what I did; I let Peter and Annelise go on their way by themselves, and I walked down the harbor road and climbed up on my rock.

Not a thing was in sight except the sea. There was an offshore wind, freshening and cold. I listened to the tide pulling at the beach, and I looked out at the miles of open water, with no foothold or handhold, and I started to feel queasy. Of course, the *Galatina* would arrive in Stockholm today, I reminded myself. Two and a half days was about now, and the weather had been good. I tried to picture the room in the inn where Aunt Dana would sleep at night. She said they all ate breakfast together at a long crowded table.

I felt better when I thought of her on land, stuck at a crowded table, and soon I jumped down and ran for home.

The next day Gunnar and Greta were late for school, so Gunnar didn't have a chance to tease me. I didn't feel like crying all day long.

That night I sat by the stove while Uncle Josef worked on his sweater. I thought it might be nice to be knitting along with him, the way other children were probably doing in their houses, and I kept remembering the knitting up in my cupboard, but I didn't want to try it.

The last time I had had that knitting out was at the end of the summer, when Aunt Dana had tried once more to teach me. She showed me a mitten with a design called "waves." Some people called the design "safe return," she said, because part way through the "wave" you loop the yarn a certain way to keep it "safe" while you finish the design, and then you "return" to start the pattern again.

"Want to see?" she had asked.

I nodded.

She put her arm around me to show me how to do it. The yarn goes on three needles, forming a triangle, and you knit with the fourth. At first I liked sitting in the circle of her arm, and I watched every stitch she took. She worked very slowly. When she had finished the "waves," they looked to me more like a row of Cs all facing right. If I blurred my eyes, I could make them look like waves.

Then she handed me the needles. Maybe this time I would catch on. My fingers felt like huge giant's fingers. I could see where to put the needle in for the first stitch, but when I pulled it through, somehow it had two strands of yarn on it instead of one. On the next stitch I came up with *three* strands, and pretty soon a long loop started to grow out from somewhere, I couldn't tell where.

"It's not working," I said.

I always made mistakes, but that wasn't the worst part. The worst part was that it gave me a terrible, lonesome closed-in feeling to sit there with the needles, trying to make obedient little stitches. I could hardly stand it.

Aunt Dana took the needles back, unknitted some stitches, knitted them up again, and handed it all back to me. "There we go," she said and gave me a pat on my wrist.

I tried some more. But now one edge of the knitting began to bend up in an odd way, and there kept on being too many stitches. Finally I pushed some of them off the needle, and a hole immediately ran down to the edge. The whole bunch of yarn seemed hateful to me. I didn't even *want* to do it right.

I had sat there knitting any old way, just sticking the needles in and out, until Aunt Dana was no longer paying attention. Then I quietly climbed the ladder to my loft and hid the tangle of yarn in my cupboard. And that's where it was going to stay.

On that first Sunday after the ship had left, Uncle Josef and I went to church, just as we always did. I passed the time by staring at the model ship that hangs from the ceiling over the altar rail. I tried to make it turn by thinking about it as hard as I could.

Afterward we said Hello and How are you? to the families who were standing around talking on the church steps.

"Ursula's a big help to you, now, isn't she?" said Magda Lagerlof to Uncle Josef. Magda's sister, Elsa, was one of the sweater ladies.

Uncle Josef nodded. "Oh, yes."

"A fine big girl, that," teased Helmut Bruzelius.

I was already as tall as Helmut was, but then he was very short. He was a carpenter in Visby and well liked by everyone. His wife's sister, Ingrid, had gone over on the *Galatina*.

I felt so good, standing there with the sun on my face, grinning at Helmut. I decided I must have already gotten past the worst part of having Aunt Dana leave.

And little by little, as each day passed, I felt more settled in without Aunt Dana. The dark dreading feeling went away. Gunnar and Greta had stopped coming to school altogether, so I didn't have to listen to Gunnar, or keep out of his way, or worry about crying. Every day I fed the chickens and gathered the eggs. Aunt Dana had shown me a long time ago how to broadcast the feed with a wide sweep of her arm, but I liked to do it my way. I threw my arm up and opened my fist all at once so the grains flew up and then showered down.

I helped lead the cows in and out of the barn. I did the washing up after meals and swept the hearth and beneath the table. I dusted the shelf where Aunt

Dana kept her special holiday dishes, and I wiped the Christmas platter every single day so it would stay perfectly clean and ready.

When Uncle Josef and I ate our evening meal, we still ate in silence. But now the silence seemed natural. And it wasn't complete silence, it was just that there was not much talk. There were plenty of ordinary household sounds: the noises of our spoons and plates, the scrape of Uncle Josef's boots, the thumps of his uneven walk around the table, the hissing of the stove.

One morning I got up extra early and searched the henhouse and found seven warm eggs. I wrapped three of them in a napkin, and while Uncle Josef was fixing breakfast I took them down the road to Anna Olafsson's house. Anna lives by herself, because she has no husband or children or any other relatives. Her front yard was thick with lavender, and red roses tumbled over the low fence, full of blooms in the October sun.

"Aren't you a good girl!" Anna exclaimed when she

opened the door. "Thank you. And I've some bundles of dye plants for you. Dana can make her blue dye when she returns. I'll bet you're missing her, aren't you. But families always make do when the sweater ladies are gone."

"Why don't you go sometime?" I asked.

"Not me. I love the comforts of home. No ships for me."

"Why not?"

She bent down and whispered, "What if it sinks?" She gave a huge laugh. "I get seasick, dearie," she added after looking into my face.

I filled my arms with the dried plants and carried them home. I wanted to run, but my legs wouldn't do it. They felt like wooden sticks.

CHAPTER FIVE

Then one day, exactly two weeks after the ship had left, Gunnar and Greta came back to school. Gunnar took up his old station, waiting for me at the schoolhouse door.

"Here's the crybaby!" he crowed as I put my foot on the bottom step. I looked up. I hadn't felt like crying for so many days I thought I was over that.

"Oh, shut up, Gunnar!" I said. But my voice sounded high and squeaky.

"The rest of us don't cry," he went on.

I knew what he meant by "the rest of us." He meant children born into island families. Not people like me.

"Shut up, I said!"

"Orphans cry!" he teased, putting his face close to mine.

I swung my lunch pail and cracked him across the head. A thick line of red blood streaked down his forehead.

"Oww!" He clamped one hand to his head. "You little witch! Help!"

Miss Nordstrom heard the commotion, of course, and came out onto the schoolhouse step. Other children gathered around.

"Let me see," said Miss Nordstrom, prying Gunnar's fingers away from his head. She frowned when she saw his scalp. "Run and get a rag from my drawer," she said to Peter Byrkind. Her gaze took in the pieces of my lunch scattered across the ground and the blue napkin from my lunch pail, caught in a bush.

"I didn't mean to do it," I squeaked out. "He was saying nasty things. He called me an orphan."

"And how is that nasty, if it's true?" asked Miss Nordstrom.

"He said it to be mean. He said I'm a crybaby, and nobody else is because they're born here."

Miss Nordstrom looked thoughtful. "Island people must endure separation at times, like all people who live by the sea. We learn through our families to be brave," she said.

Her words felt like icy stones hitting me. So even she thought I wasn't like the other children.

"Gunnar, you have better things to do than tease younger children. Go in now and sit at your seat and press this rag hard on the cut. You will stay at your desk for the rest of the day. Ursula, you must go home and think over the consequences of letting your temper get the best of you. Now pick up your lunch. I shall look for you tomorrow."

Annelise's eyes opened wide. Hardly anyone was ever sent home from school. Greta tugged at my sleeve and whispered in my ear, "Gunnar gets like this when Mama is away." Then she darted off.

"Ursula?" Miss Nordstrom prompted.

"Yes, Miss Nordstrom." The words came out all

high and mooing, because I was crying so hard, and I turned my back so that no one could see. The ground was blurry as I picked up the rolls and a piece of cheese and the blue cloth. I set off without another word. But I didn't go straight home. When I was out of sight of the school, I walked the half mile out to my rock.

I stood on top of it for a minute, shivering and still hiccupping. Then I sat down, tucked my skirt in close to keep my legs warm, and I looked out far past the harbor and cried.

I dreaded to think what Uncle Josef would say when he found out I had been sent home from school. By tonight everyone would know.

Why did Miss Nordstrom have to say that, in front of everyone? *We learn through our families to be brave. We* learn through our families to be brave, but *you* haven't learned that.

I listened to the tide as it washed back and forth over the sand. Finally the last of the crying was smoothed away.

Maybe I *was* a crybaby. I hated to think that stupid Gunnar could be right about anything, especially about me.

But maybe I was. Well, so what. I was different from the island people, and I would just *stay* different. As soon as I was older, I would go back to Stockholm and live all alone in the fine big house that had belonged to my parents. Though someone else must live in it now. I couldn't remember the house myself, but Aunt Dana had told me it was large. Sometimes I imagined the painted furniture, the bright rugs and embroidered pillows.

I couldn't remember anything about my parents, either, except that once my mother had been picking flowers in a field and she handed me a big bouquet. I had buried my face in it, and I could still see the blue and yellow flowers; but the features of my mother's face were vague, and nothing could bring them back.

I wondered if my mother had ever been a crybaby, or if she would be ashamed to know that I was.

I reached into my lunch pail and pulled out a roll. I brushed off a leaf that clung to it and took a bite.

Then I remembered the worm of blood running down Gunnar's face, and I felt terrible. I could still feel the solid *crack* when the pail had hit his head.

I put away the rest of my roll and stood up. I was shivering in the cold, and a fine mist was moving rapidly onto land. I picked my way home in the fog, my lunch pail hanging heavy in my hand.

Uncle Josef didn't come back to the cottage until late that afternoon. I spent most of the day watching the chickens and going for walks up and down the pastures. When at last he came in, I was sitting at the table, waiting.

Uncle Josef pulled a pot of stew onto the front part of the stove and took some bread out of the cupboard. I hoped he would ask me what was wrong, but he didn't notice. I gave a noisy sigh and got to my feet and set the table. I sighed again and sat down with a *thunk*.

"Miss Nordstrom sent me home from school today," I said finally.

After a moment Uncle Josef said, "Why?"

"I hit Gunnar with my lunch pail, and his head started to bleed."

"Why did you do such a thing?" Uncle Josef's voice was calm, more curious than alarmed.

"He teases me. Every day he calls me a crybaby, and today he said people born on this island don't cry, and I'm a crybaby orphan. So I hit him."

"Then you must go apologize."

I looked at Uncle Josef. "No! I won't!"

"You must apologize for hitting him."

"Then he has to apologize, too."

"That is up to him. But you must do what is right. Tomorrow Hans is lending me his cart. We will drive it to the Helfrigs' farm after school."

"But I don't want to!"

"I will come with you," said Uncle Josef, and that was that.

The next day there was no Gunnar waiting by the schoolhouse door, and he and Greta disappeared after lunch and didn't come back. Miss Nordstrom acted as if nothing had happened the day before.

"Are you cross about something?" Annelise asked me as we started home. She hadn't asked me any questions on the way to school, and I hadn't given her any tidbits. I knew she was dying to know whether Uncle Josef had punished me. I suppose I was scowling. "What did your uncle say?" she pried in a delicate voice.

"About what?"

"You know. Yesterday."

"Oh, nothing."

The cart was waiting in front of the cottage. I bumped along in silence beside Uncle Josef. Soon we left the main path and went down a narrow lane, and at the end of that I could see a small house. I had never been here. As we drove up, a couple of dusty chickens in the road squawked and scrambled out of our way. A pig was rooting by the front step. Uncle Josef stopped the cart and climbed down. I jumped to the ground and followed him to the front door, standing just behind him. He knocked and called out, "Hello? Hello?"

At first we heard nothing; then slow footsteps, and the door was pulled open a crack.

I peeped around Uncle Josef and saw Greta's face in the narrow space.

"Who's here?" Uncle Josef asked.

Greta opened the door. "Just me and my brother. Auntie Birgit went home sick."

We stepped in. The room was dim, and household things were strewn everywhere, as if no one had tidied up for days. There were dishes sitting on the table with bits of dried food on them, and a pot with something burned black inside it. A heap of bedding had been thrown on the floor. Gunnar came slouching down the ladder from the loft. He looked as if he had just woken up.

"Go on, now," said Uncle Josef, giving me a nudge.

Gunnar's eyes narrowed when he saw me, as if he was ready to continue the fight.

"I am sorry I hit you with the pail and hurt your head," I said. There. It was out. It wasn't so bad doing it with Uncle Josef standing right behind me.

"Yes, well," said Gunnar. He looked about him. "I told Greta to tidy up, but she won't obey."

"I tried to! I can't do everything!" Greta said.

"Auntie is supposed to come back, but we don't know when."

"We'll be on our way, then," said Uncle Josef.

We went back outside to the cart. Greta ran up to me as I was climbing in. "See if you can find out when Auntie will be better," she whispered.

Uncle Josef turned the cart around, and we bounced along the uneven path back to the main road. "I'll have a word with Anna Olafsson about this," he said. "Someone must go over there."

I jumped down from the cart when we reached our cottage. Uncle Josef drove on toward Anna Olafsson's house, and I went in and put out the plates for supper. When Uncle Josef returned, he said Anna had promised to go straight over to try to right things in the Helfrigs' household. She would bring the children some food and stay the night, and tomorrow she would see if Auntie Birgit was well enough to come back.

"What if their aunt won't come?" I asked.

"Someone will look out for them, now that we know," said Uncle Josef.

"I wonder why Gunnar is so mean," I said.

"He has no father to teach him, no uncles either," said Uncle Josef. "And perhaps a troll watched over his birth."

CHAPTER SIX

It was not until the third Sunday after the ship had left that people began to talk about when the sweater ladies might come back. It was a warm day, the way it will sometimes be in early November, and Uncle Josef and I were standing outside after church. "We can start to look for them after one more sermon," joked Magda Lagerlof. She laughed. "My sister's sweaters must all be sold by now!"

"And no storms yet this year," said Anna Olafsson.

"As long as there have been ships there have been storms," said Anselm Knutson, who was always gloomy. He and his mother raised sheep on a farm near us, and Aunt Dana said she was one of the finest knitters on the island.

"But the ship's a new one, and very seaworthy," said Magda.

"The captain's an old one, and very seaworthy, too," said Helmut Bruzelius.

And then four weeks were up.

"The ship will come today!" I said to Uncle Josef at breakfast.

"It's no good expecting it till it's in," said Uncle Josef.

"But it's been four weeks. That's enough time!"

"Some years, yes, some years, no," said Uncle Josef.

I went straight to my rock after school and sat there for a long time. Twice I saw a shape on the horizon, something dark and tall, like the mast of a ship. But both times it wavered and then was gone in a moment, like a twist of smoke.

The ship didn't come that day.

The next day on the way home from school I looked out from my rock again. No ship, and something had made the water look different. It was a lighter color with small waves racing every which way on top and big patches of darker water moving slowly underneath.

Some men stopped by the cottage late in the afternoon. They said they had been down by the harbor and had noticed that the air felt heavy and the water was choppy. They warned Uncle Josef to be sure his barn was secure in case it began to blow.

That evening the first storm hit. I lay in my loft close under the roof and listened to the wild beating of sheets of rain. I could still hear Anselm Knutson's gloomy voice —*As long as there have been ships there have been storms.* But maybe there was good weather in Stockholm; and if there was a storm, Aunt Dana's ship would stay in port until it was safe to leave. She had said so.

By morning the storm was gone, and a warm pink sunrise lay over the island. Our fence gate had been torn off, and a stiff wind kept blowing all day. After school Annelise and Peter and I went down to the harbor. The storm was still in the churning water, light green and dirty, full of seaweed and foam and sand and chunks of wood.

"Are those pieces of a ship?" Peter asked.

"I hope not," said Annelise, sneaking a look at me.

"If a ship is out in a storm, what happens to it?" I asked at suppertime.

Uncle Josef pursed his lips. "A ship's captain knows all weathers," he said finally.

"Aunt Dana's ship — it wouldn't leave in a storm, would it?"

"Not unless the captain's a fool," said Uncle Josef.

"If they had already started, they would go back, wouldn't they?"

"If the captain decides so," said Uncle Josef. "And if it is possible."

"But now the storm is over, isn't it?" I said.

"In autumn there is never only one storm." Uncle Josef lit his pipe and stared off into a corner of the room.

A few days later another storm swept over the island, and this one lasted for three days. We stayed indoors, except for once or twice when Uncle Josef went out to the barn. He wouldn't let me go with him, the wind was so strong.

On the evening of the third day, someone hammered on our door. It was Helmut Bruzelius. "I've come to tell you—a ship has broken up outside the harbor, but it's not the *Galatina*."

Helmut stepped in and stood by the stove, water pouring from his clothes. Drops kept hissing as they hit the hot iron. "There were no passengers and only a small crew. The *Oslo*. They rowed ashore."

"Where did they start out?" asked Uncle Josef.

"Stockholm."

Both men were silent.

"And?" Uncle Josef said finally.

"The captain said the *Galatina* set out five days before the *Oslo*."

"So." Uncle Josef pressed his hand against the table, and I saw that his arm was trembling. "But no definite word."

Helmut shook his head. "I'm going on now. I don't want others to get the wrong news." He ducked out into the night.

Uncle Josef continued to lean on the table. "It is early yet," he said, almost to himself. "Only a few days late."

"It could come in tomorrow," I said. "Or the day after that."

"It could," said Uncle Josef.

The next day I walked over to the Gunderssons' with a couple of freshly laid eggs. I had found only two in the henhouse, because the storm had upset the chickens. Everywhere the ground was littered with branches torn from trees. A cold strong wind was blowing.

Marta gave me a quick squeeze around the shoulders as she took the eggs. She looked worried.

"There was a shipwreck, but it wasn't the *Galatina*," I said.

"So we heard," said Marta. "We're so thankful it wasn't the *Galatina*."

Annelise and Peter were sitting at breakfast, and they watched me without saying anything.

"It will come in any day, maybe even today," I said.

"This is the longest they've ever been gone," said a dry voice from the dark corner by the hearth.

"Oh, no, Mother," said Marta. "Some years they've taken many more days than—"

"My Olaf died at sea," Granny interrupted. "That's what happened to him. Lost at sea."

"Yes, Mother, now let's not dwell on it," said Marta.

"Never saw him again. Never found his body." Granny was missing several teeth, so that her lips folded in, and this gave her face an expression of finality.

"Yes, Mother. Ursula's aunt is on the ship coming back, you know. Any day now we're hoping to see her."

"Sometimes the sweater is all they have to go by. A fisherman drowns, his body washes up, and that's the only way they can tell who it is — the pattern in the sweater. But nobody ever found Olaf." Her voice trembled and cracked.

A dark sick feeling settled in my stomach.

"Thank you for the eggs, Ursula," said Marta, putting an arm around me and steering me toward the door.

On that Sunday when we walked into church people looked at Uncle Josef and me with solemn faces. As we moved along the bench to our places I heard a woman saying, "—must have broken up. Nothing could survive in those seas." I suddenly pictured Aunt Dana being carried down in the foaming green water. We sat down in front of the woman, and she stopped talking. Inga Wilhelmsson, whose mother had also gone, came in late with her father, and when she saw everyone watching them, she burst into tears. The church was absolutely quiet, except for Inga's crying and her father's footsteps ringing on the wooden floor.

The minister got up and prayed for the ship at sea. He said we had to remember "the pillars of our faith" and accept God's will. It made me shiver to think of the cold pillars. And what did he mean about God's will? God's will couldn't possibly be for the ship to be lost. Could it? How could God *want* the ship to sink?

I couldn't stand to stay for the hymns and long prayers and even longer sermon that I knew was coming. As the congregation rustled to its feet for yet another hymn with seven verses, I slipped past Uncle Josef and walked quickly down the side aisle and out the door.

The sun was bleak, a pale yellow disk shining through thin gray clouds, but even a watered-down sun was warmer than church. I ran to my rock. The sight from the top was so awful I jumped right back down again. Waves raced in, crashed, were sucked out with a steady roar. Nothing could come in on that wild water.

I ran home. I went into the cottage and stood with my eyes shut in the center of the room, catching my breath. My head was churning like the water. I tried to calm myself by thinking back to when Aunt Dana was there every day. What were the sounds she usually made? I couldn't remember. I could only hear Uncle Josef's heavy boots unevenly thumping on the floor.

I opened my eyes. The more I tried to remember

Aunt Dana, the more my memory skittered away like one of our stupid chickens.

I closed my eyes again, and then something did come to me. I remembered how it felt when Aunt Dana had put her arms around me to show me how to work the knitting needles.

I climbed the ladder to the loft and pulled open the cupboard drawer. There it was, the tangle of yarn with the needles sticking out every which way. It looked reassuringly solid and homey, even comical, like a little household troll — "I'm still here, you can't get rid of me!"

I climbed back down with it and sat at one end of the table. I turned the knitting around and looked at it from all sides. It was a mess. I had no idea how to fix it, but I could start over. Maybe if I went very slowly, one stitch at a time, I could keep away the bad feeling.

I pulled out the needles and laid them side by side on the table. Then I began to rip out the stitches. It was slow going, because there were hard knots, and I was not about to break the yarn and bring bad luck. At last the final row came out with a single satisfying ripple. I wound the kinked yarn onto the two balls, one white, one dark gray, and put them far apart on the table. Then I took up one of the double-pointed needles. One thing I *could* remember was how to cast on.

Over your thumb and forefinger, then dip the needle around and through: over and over, until I had enough cast-on stitches. Then one by one I slipped them onto three needles to form a triangle. Now came the hard part. I threaded the yarn through my fingers, picked up the fourth needle, and tried to knit the first stitch. "Keep it loose," Aunt Dana always said. Right away the yarn around my fingers tightened up. I shook my hand free, rewound the yarn around my fingers, and tried again. The smooth wooden needles, miraculously, did not fall out of the stitches. And, almost by accident, the yarn began to move along in little tugs, the way it was supposed to.

After I had gone around once, a long loop of yarn suddenly opened up in the row of stitches, and my heart lurched. The loop wasn't supposed to be there. It wasn't going to happen again, my getting all mixed up. It couldn't. I looked carefully, and then I took another stitch, and a long end pulled through, and the loop was gone. I went on.

Aunt Dana would really smile if she could see this.

By the time Uncle Josef came home from church, I had done two complete rounds, and the stitches were in the right order — gray, gray, white, gray, gray, white. I didn't know what he would say to me about leaving church. But he didn't give me even one disapproving look. "So here you are," he said, and went about preparing our lunch.

In the morning I began to work on the next round of the pattern. I tried to hear Aunt Dana's voice telling me what to do next. It would take eight rows to complete the curve that was the wave, the safe return. I gulped down my breakfast so fast it nearly stuck in my throat.

As I was finishing the fourth round Annelise and Peter called from the path, "Are you ready? Come on, Ursula!"

I shouted out the door, "Don't wait for me — I'll catch up with you."

By the end of the sixth round, though, I was in trouble. Part of each wave was ahead of where it should have been, and the waves looked broken.

I left the knitting on the table, grabbed my lunch pail, and ran all the way to school. Miss Nordstrom gave me a look that said, *Don't think I haven't noticed you're late,* but she didn't scold me. She knew very well which of us had mothers or aunts on the *Galatina.*

The Olson twins sat like scared little birds and said nothing all day. At lunchtime Nils Ekstrom fell off the lowest step, and even though he's as old as I am, he held his knee and bawled. Miss Nordstrom put her arms around him; nobody laughed. Clouds began to gather again.

Annelise invited me to come home with her after school. I looked for their granny in the corner by the hearth, but her chair was empty. A snore came from a room behind the chimney. Annelise and

Peter and I began to giggle, until Marta shushed us —
"Be quiet! Do you want her to wake up?"

No one mentioned the *Galatina*. Marta rolled out
gingerbread dough on a floured board. We cut out
cookie men and women and pressed in raisins for eyes
and buttons. Annelise and Peter were acting as giddy
as maywheels. They kept chasing each other around the
table and going off into peals of laughter.

"Go outside if you must carry on," said Marta,
shooing us out the door. The sky was black with
swollen clouds, but that only made us laugh more.
We chased one another around and around the
house, stumbling and gasping, until the cookies were
done and Marta called us in. She let us each take
one. I crammed mine into my mouth, and while I
was rolling it around on my tongue to cool it, Peter
blurted out, "Father says the *Galatina* won't come
back. He says it's sunk in the sea."

"Shhh!" Annelise hissed at him.

"Peter! What did I say?" Marta scolded.

But it was too late, the words were out.

All the laughter had stopped.

"Your father doesn't know," I said stubbornly. But now I was afraid, so afraid, and the fear rolled across me like the wild waves at the foot of my rock. "I think I want to go home."

"Take some cookies with you," said Marta. She filled a napkin with warm ginger cookies, twisted the corners into a knot, and put it in my hand. "Run along quickly now, or you'll get soaked." She patted me on the shoulder, then suddenly she pressed me against her shawl in an awkward hug. Her eyes had tears in them.

I ran as fast as I ever had in my life. I didn't care about the rain; I ran so that I didn't feel anything but my feet pounding and my lungs hurting for air. I heard the crack and sizzle of lightning over my head as I pushed open the cottage door. Uncle Josef had set the table and was poking a wooden spoon into something in the big iron pot. I stood there gasping for breath, then I threw myself face down onto the bench and hid my face in my arms. "Peter says his father says the *Galatina* won't come back," I said.

I heard the spoon knock against the side of the pot.

"Some people are saying that," said Uncle Josef.

"It's not true, is it?" I waited for his answer, still hiding my face.

"God doesn't tell us what *will* happen, or what will not," Uncle Josef said after a moment.

The wind picked up, and the rain beat down.

After we had eaten, I took out the mitten. I pulled out three rows, stitch by stitch, and started around again. The pattern had to be exactly right. I finished four rounds, this time with no mistakes.

"So we have a knitter after all, do we?" said Uncle Josef. He stirred the fire, sat down in his chair, and picked up his gulls sweater.

The next morning I finished the last four rows. A gale was blowing outside, but I didn't listen. I smoothed the knitted fabric with my thumb, just the way Aunt Dana did, and held it out to look at it. Everything went clockwise, as it was supposed to; there were no knots, no broken strands. Each wave curled upon the next wave, like a tide heading into shore. I would keep knitting these waves, I would knit them and knit them and knit them, until the ship came home.

CHAPTER SEVEN

We had storms for yet another two weeks, on into December, and snow blew down with the rain. Now the *Galatina* was a whole month overdue, long enough for the women to have made the entire journey there and back all over again. No ships at all came into the harbor, so there was no one to bring us news. At school Miss Nordstrom tried to keep our minds on our lessons, but she had stopped scolding when someone forgot a recitation, and she allowed us to do the same geography lesson three days in a row. Each night I sat by Uncle Josef and did a few more rows on my mitten.

One afternoon Uncle Josef borrowed the Gunderssons' cart, and we got ready to go to Helga Hanson's house. A cold winter fog had closed around the house, so we had to wrap ourselves in heavy blankets. Uncle Josef did the driving. "I'm fetching something, and you never mind what," he said.

Helga opened the door for us. She had been working her spinning wheel, with her baby sleeping in a cradle by her foot.

"It's ready for you," she said. She went to a shelf and took down a bundle wrapped in canvas and handed it to Uncle Josef. "Dana will like this," she said. Her voice sounded too loud and bright, and I heard fear threading through her words.

Uncle Josef pulled out some coins and put them into Helga's hand.

"No, I can't let you," she said, trying to give them back.

"We settled on the price," said Uncle Josef. He folded his arms and tucked his hands underneath them.

Helga's husband came into the room. "Many have given them up, Josef," he said abruptly.

Uncle Josef gave me a sidelong glance. "Some, yes."

Henrik frowned. "Very bad storms, I hear that. Very bad."

"Henrik — the child." Helga placed her hand on his arm.

We bundled ourselves up again and climbed back into the cart and started for home. By the time we had gone a few yards down the road, the Hansons' cottage had vanished in the fog. I wished I could make Henrik's words vanish, too.

When we got home, Uncle Josef put the package in the room behind the chimney, where he and Aunt Dana slept.

I went straight over and picked up my knitting. I had finished three complete lines of waves in the mitten by now, and I showed them to Uncle Josef.

"Very fine," he said. "So where is the thumb?"

The next day after school I went home with Annelise and Peter again and asked Marta about thumbs.

"What about them?"

"How do you make them? If you happen to be knitting a mitten?"

Marta's mouth opened and closed, as if she started to say something and then changed her mind. "I'll show you," she said. She pulled out some yarn and knitted up the beginnings of a mitten cuff. "Look here." She put some of the stitches onto a separate piece of yarn, then she went on knitting around and around, right past them. "When you get to the very end, you come back and knit up the thumb."

"Thank you!" I dashed out the door and raced home before I could forget what Marta had shown me. The thumb on my mitten was going to start high up, but that didn't matter. This mitten was just going to have a very long cuff.

Once I was past that, the knitting was easier. I could go around and around without having to think so much. I tried to work on it every day, even if it was only a few stitches. I didn't want it finished too soon. And I didn't want anyone but Uncle Josef to know about it. Annelise or Marta might pick it up and change something for me, and it had to be all my own work, every stitch. I hid it whenever I heard someone coming to the cottage door.

Sometimes I hid myself, too. No matter who it was, visitors always said something about the *Galatina.* So I went out to the barn and stood in the warm darkness, where I didn't have to hear anything.

Now the ship was a month and a week late.

"When will we go get the Christmas pole?" I asked Uncle Josef.

"The Christmas pole? I hadn't thought to do that."

A grove of spruce trees stands at one boundary of my aunt and uncle's farm. The trees are too crowded there to grow big and fat, and we can always find a nice tall skinny one without many branches. Uncle Josef chops it down and we take it home and twine branches of greenery around it and set it up in front of the house. Sometimes we're the first ones on the island to put ours up.

"Aunt Dana will wonder why we haven't done it yet," I said.

Uncle Josef looked at me, and for such a long time, that I finally found my coat and went out alone. "I'm going to look for one!" I called back.

I was there in a few minutes. Even though they were thin, the trees sheltered the grove from the wind, and the spruce needles made a carpet of silence beneath my feet. I walked to the center and looked up. It felt like a magical place, with straight slim trees reaching all the way to heaven. Any one of these would do. I closed my eyes and turned around a few times and took a step, waving my hands in front of my face to make sure I didn't crash into anything. As soon as I touched a piece of bark, I chose that one. I opened my eyes. Someone was standing nearby, watching me.

"Gunnar!" I said. "What are you doing, standing there like a ghost?"

"I sometimes come here," he said. "It's like a church, but no one telling you to be good."

"I don't like church much."

"I hate it. I won't go. This place is better, and if there is any God to hear us, the prayers go up better from here."

If there is any God? I had never heard such talk in my life.

"You won't tell anyone I come here, will you?" Gunnar said.

I shook my head. I couldn't tell from looking at him what mood he was in, but he had never asked anything of me before. "Were you sending up prayers?" I said.

"Never you mind." The old mean look crossed his face, then vanished.

"I'm picking out a tree for our Christmas pole," I said.

"Are you crazy?"

My heart started to pound. "What makes you say that?" I asked, though I knew exactly why he had said that.

"Nothing can help them, they're gone!" Gunnar shouted.

"No!" I shrieked at him.

Our harsh voices shattered the silence like an ax smashing through glass. I was trembling, and so was he, the big oaf.

"They can still come back," I whispered, fear bubbling up in me everywhere. *No knots, everything going to the left, not a missed stitch.* The words ran over and over through my head. I had done everything I knew to keep away bad luck.

Gunnar put his hands on my shoulders, and I was afraid he was going to shake me in anger. Instead he firmed up his grip and gave my shoulders a comforting squeeze.

"Yes," he said, breathing rapidly. "Okay. They can still come back."

Then he turned and ran away, out of the grove and across the field till he was lost to view.

I tied a length of yarn around the tree trunk and walked home. "I've found one," I said to Uncle Josef.

Uncle Josef gave out a sigh. "Ursula, how can we?" he said.

"We *have* to."

"It wouldn't be right, now. Some have put on mourning."

Something started to press hard inside my chest. "We have to! *We have to!*" I was suddenly shouting.

"Oh, my." Uncle Josef took my hand in his and patted it. "Well, now, let's go then, before I finish up in the barn."

We covered the distance slowly. I stood out of the way as Uncle Josef gave the tree trunk several cuts with his ax. It fell just where he wanted it to, and after he had trimmed off the branches, we dragged it back across the fields together. After Uncle Josef finished with the barn animals, we draped greenery around the tree trunk and propped it up in front of the house. Lightly falling snow gave the Christmas pole a dusting of sparkles.

"There." I stood back to see the effect. Uncle Josef looked so sad, I thought then that I had probably made a mistake. "Aunt Dana will love to see this when she gets home," I said, but my voice came out so pinched and shaky even I could hardly understand the words.

"Yes, she will," said Uncle Josef. He looked down at me, and his voice was steady.

CHAPTER EIGHT

Then the weather began to clear. For two days the sun stayed out, and I could see from my rock that the water had settled down.

"Better sailing now," I said to Uncle Josef. I was holding open the barn door while he shooed out the cows.

He turned away from me to fasten the barn door, and he didn't speak or look back as he followed the cows out to the pasture. I ran away in the opposite direction to the sheep fields. I dug my fingers into one old sheep's back and yanked hard on her coat. She let out a bleat and shied away from me. I followed her and gave her a kick, and this time she scampered far out of my reach. I sat down and took a stick and jabbed it over and over into the scrubby ground until it broke.

Then I sat there for a long time.

Still no ships came in, not the *Galatina*, not any ship.

The Sunday before Christmas, Anselm Knutson was the last to come out of church. He stood on the top step and looked down at the rest of us. He waved his hand at the blue sky. "Too late now," he said, shaking his head and muttering to himself. Then he climbed into his cart and drove away.

That night I had gone to bed, and Uncle Josef was still sitting by the stove, when a heavy knock came at the door. "Josef? I must talk to you." It was Helmut Bruzelius. I slipped out of bed and crouched by the top of the ladder.

"There can be no hope for them now," Helmut said. "I and some others have been talking to the minister. They could not have been on the sea all this time, no matter how much we have been hoping. We have to have a service for them, a funeral service."

"I see," said Uncle Josef.

"They're talking of having it the day after Christmas," said Helmut. "I'll come by again tomorrow. I am sorry, Josef."

I crawled back into bed and lay there shivering. Then I got up again and climbed down the ladder.

"I heard Helmut," I said. "Are they going to have that service?"

"Maybe."

"I'm not going," I said.

"Ah."

I sat down at the end of the table and picked up my unfinished mitten. I knitted another row of waves, and then it was time to finish the hand part. I threaded the yarn through the last few stitches and pulled them close. I turned the mitten inside out and wove in the loose end with a sewing needle. Now there was only the thumb to go.

Uncle Josef got up and draped a shawl around my shoulders. I kept on, even though my fingers got tired and as stiff as twigs on a tree. At last I had finished the thumb. "Look," I said. I held up the mitten, free of the needles, completely done, pretty much perfect.

Uncle Josef nodded.

I went to sit beside him, and we were quiet for some minutes. I spread the mitten out flat on my knee. "Aunt Dana showed me this pattern," I said. "It's called two different names, either 'waves' or 'safe return.'"

Uncle Josef looked down at me. "'Safe return,' eh?" he said.

"See?" I held the mitten up again for his inspection.

"Yes," he said. "I do see." But he didn't seem to be looking at the mitten.

Uncle Josef didn't say anything to me the next day or the day after that. We did our chores and tended the animals, and he kept the fire going in the stove, but he forgot to cook food for us. I had to ask him to put on water to boil, and I made the porridge and our supper soup as well.

Maybe his leg was hurting, I thought. If it was, he wouldn't say anything about it. But he walked around the house and in and out of the barn the way he usually did. I was afraid of what his silence really meant. I was afraid that even Uncle Josef had finally given up. I began to wish that I hadn't finished the mitten, that I could still sit down with it and knit a few more rows.

And then it was Christmas Eve. This was the darkest time of the year, when the sun came up latest, and I waited until I could see a little light in the sky before I got up. Uncle Josef had wakened long before and was sitting on his chair, looking at the floor. When I came down my ladder, he got to his feet and began to stir up the fire.

"Tomorrow is Christmas," I said.

"So it is." On Christmas Eve every other year the room was bright with Christmas hangings and straw decorations, and the house smelled of ginger and cinnamon all day long. We had a painted wooden bird that Aunt Dana usually hung over the table, and it turned in the drafts. It had a chip in its beak, where it had fallen one year. Today the room was plain and bare, as if the holiday itself had died.

I pulled on my jacket and went out to feed the chickens. The sky was beginning to show the colors of sunrise, and I looked up to see which stars were still shining. Then a breeze blew across my face, and I smelled the evergreen boughs tied to the Christmas pole; the damp air had made them fragrant. It was Christmas, and Aunt Dana wasn't here. There was no Christmas at all. And there was no Aunt Dana. Maybe never would be again. I suddenly felt sick.

I unfastened the henhouse door to let out the chickens. Now all the things people had said came rushing through my ears, the things I hadn't wanted to hear —

Nothing could survive in those seas . . .

There can be no hope for them now . . .

I am sorry, Josef.

"No, no," I heard myself say out loud. The hens tilted their heads this way and that, as if they were interested. "No," I said again. Somehow I had to keep away the sick sliding feeling that was pulling at me.

I reached into the feed bin and threw out a handful of grain. I was cold all over, and shaking, and my hand felt like a piece of wood. The chickens rushed past my ankles, clucking and squawking, and then I heard something. I heard a bell ring far away. I stopped everything, frozen like ice, and listened. "Shush up," I commanded the chickens. It was a church bell in Visby.

The bell kept ringing, and in a moment more bells joined in, and then more and more. All the cathedrals in Visby must have suddenly come awake. My heart knew the sense of it right away. When bad news came, there was only one bell ringing — one slow, mournful bell.

I dashed back inside the cottage.

"You go as fast as you can," said Uncle Josef, already reaching for his walking stick. "I'll come right along."

I ran, ran, ran. Other islanders were coming from all directions, hurrying toward the harbor at Visby. A knot of people had gathered on a slope overlooking the city walls. "Ursula, Ursula, look!" they cried to me. "Look!" They pointed out over the walls toward the water. A ship was coming in.

Helmut Bruzelius stood nearby with his wife and children, and next to them huddled his sister-in-law's family — the husband, Peter Larson, and their two little girls. Helmut was looking through a spyglass. Everyone else had their eyes on the approaching ship, tense and silent.

"What if it's not the *Galatina*?" asked Helmut's son, Karl.

"In a moment we will know," said Helmut.

"Who else would come in now?" His daughter, Maria, stamped her foot impatiently. "We've been waiting all this time!"

Helmut's wife ignored them and only watched the sea.

"Yes!" shouted Helmut. "I can see it! The flag! Here, look for yourself!" He handed the glass to Peter Larson. Peter looked and immediately bowed his head and pressed his hand against his eyes.

Gunnar and Greta ran up then, Gunnar dragging Greta by the hand.

"Gunnar!" shouted Helmut. "See here, give him the glass! Look, my boy, look! It's the *Galatina*!"

Uncle Josef and I waited forever at the dock as the ship slowly moved through the harbor to its berthing spot. I kept squinting, straining my eyes to see the figures on the deck. And there she was, there she really was. I waved frantically. I gripped Uncle Josef's hand and looked up at him and saw that his eyes were full of tears.

At last I wrapped my arms around Aunt Dana's waist, and Aunt Dana was hugging me and Uncle Josef at the same time, all of us stepping on each other's toes in a joyous tangle of arms and cheeks and kisses. "We were blown off course, we landed in Estonia," said Aunt Dana. "We were there for weeks, and no way to let you know that we were safe. The captain refused to set out again until last week."

All around us other families were hugging and exclaiming, crying and laughing —

"Are you all right?"

"By the grace of God!"

"A miracle!"

Gunnar and Greta and their mother were swaying from side to side, their arms entwined around each other's shoulders. I saw that even Gunnar had tears running down his cheeks.

The bells rang on, children whooped and sang and danced around. Grownups would laugh and shout one minute, and the next stop and clasp their hands and pronounce a prayer, and then they would begin to weep again.

Finally everyone was laughing more than they were crying, and families began to gather up the women's traveling things and start for home.

"Just in time for Christmas, eh?" Sonja Wilhelmsson called out to Aunt Dana as they parted. "What did I tell you?"

"Now we can have Christmas!" I said when we reached our cottage.

While Uncle Josef heated some soup, Aunt Dana and I went into the back room to open the chest where the Christmas things were stored. Aunt Dana lifted out the tapestries, and there underneath was the canvas bundle that Uncle Josef was going to give her. She pretended not to see it.

In no time we had fastened the tapestries up around the walls, and once more the wise men in red and purple robes journeyed across the desert; an infant Jesus reached up from his yellow straw. Aunt Dana took down the Christmas platter. "You've kept this so clean, I don't even have to wipe it," she said. I placed the big Christmas candlestick in the center of the table, and Aunt Dana dug into the bottom of her bag and brought up three stout red candles. Uncle Josef fitted them into the holders and lit them, and we all said, "Ah!"

Later on we heard knocks and shouts at the door, and in came Hans and Marta and Annelise and Peter. Now it was their turn to exclaim and cry. They had brought us creamed herring and saffron rolls and gingerbread and the special sausage Hans always makes for Christmas.

"I knew it hadn't sunk," said Peter.

"And she brought the red candles," said Annelise.

That night I didn't eat much, and neither did Uncle Josef, but Aunt Dana said she hadn't been dining so well lately, and she made up for both of us.

"Did you sell everything?" asked Uncle Josef.

Aunt Dana nodded. "All but two sweaters, and luckily I had them to wear. We were terribly cold on the ship."

"Did you have any mittens?" I asked.

"I was able to borrow some, thank goodness."

"And did you find treasures in the marketplace like last year?" I asked. "Did you bring anything back?"

"Tomorrow is time enough for that," said Aunt Dana. "So much for one day!"

"But it's Christmas Eve," I said. "And I have a present. Something that will really surprise you."

"Oh, all right."

I raced up the ladder to my loft and opened the cupboard drawer. I pulled out the mitten, looked it over one last time, and tucked it into my skirt pocket. By the time I had scrambled back down, Aunt Dana had cleared away the dishes and put her tapestry bag on the table.

First she pulled out a shiny new ax head. "For you, Josef. Something you have been needing. And something else." She took out a linen shirt embroidered with birds and handed it to him.

"This is for Ursula." She held out a silver bracelet with a clasp held by a tiny silver chain. I put it around my wrist. The silver glowed and caught the light from the candles. "And I know you were waiting for this!" Aunt Dana pulled out a paper packet that rattled when she shook it.

"I can guess!" I said. Candy, at least a hundred pieces, of all sorts — peppermint, taffy, cinnamon.

"And this is my present to you, Dana." Uncle Josef handed her the canvas bundle. Aunt Dana unfolded the covering and took a deep breath. It was a blanket finely woven of creamy white wool. She brought a corner of it up to her cheek. "As soft as down," she said.

"And now, for Ursula." Uncle Josef went into the bedroom again and this time brought out something made of gleaming wood — a yarn winder. Every turn was perfectly smooth, every joint perfectly fitted.

"Aha. Perhaps you will use that someday," said Aunt Dana tactfully.

"Yes, yes, I will," I said. "Wait till you see my present for you." I reached into my pocket and pulled out the mitten.

Aunt Dana looked at it, and a smile moved slowly across her face. "You made this?" she asked. I nodded. "It's beautiful." She slipped it onto one hand and turned it every which way. It reached nearly to her elbow. "Even the thumb is perfect, and the long cuff will be so warm."

"No one helped me, either."

"Wait till I show Marta."

"Yes!"

"So you did it all by yourself."

"Yes!"

"But what about the other mitten?"

"Oops!" I started to laugh, and so did Uncle Josef and Aunt Dana.

"It's so beautiful, I will surely want a pair."

"Oh, no! Uncle Josef! I forgot!" I hadn't thought about anything but finishing the mitten. "I don't have anything to give you!"

"You gave me something already," said Uncle Josef.

A while after that Aunt Dana said I had to go to sleep. "Good night, and God bless," said Uncle Josef.

I nodded and climbed up to my loft. After I got into bed I heard them continuing to talk below; Uncle Josef laughed at something Aunt Dana told him. Through the tiny window by my bed I could see light snow falling, giving the fields a soft glittering layer of white. I pulled the feather bed up to my nose. I thought of Gunnar then, in the spruce grove; I thought of myself knitting like everyone else, probably even while I was walking to school with Annelise. If I got really good. If I really wanted to. And one day I would go to Stockholm and see my old house, but I would come back here afterward. I belonged here. Of course Aunt Dana would say I always had, but it felt different now. I kept seeing the gray-and-white mitten as I fell asleep — the alternating stitches, now dark, now light, shaping themselves into rows of waves, into a safe return, a safe return, a safe return.

Author's Note

This story is based on a real incident described in the introduction to The Swedish Mitten Book: Traditional Patterns from Gotland, *by Inger Gottfridsson and Ingrid Gottfridsson (English translation © 1984 by Lark Books, Asheville, North Carolina). In the fall of 1824, the ship carrying the "sweaterhags" of Gotland on their return trip from Stockholm encountered a terrible storm and was blown far off course. The ship arrived on Christmas Eve, weeks after it had been given up for lost.*